Shema and Rick: The First Experience In Lust

A Seshat Hathor Creation

Copyright © 2018 Seshat Hathor

All rights reserved.

ISBN-10: 1724645560
ISBN-13: 978-1724645562

DEDICATION

To my four daughters: NyNy, Ari, Tummy and Zuzu, I can't WAIT to experience all of life's joys with you girls. You deserve the world and MORE. Let me create one for you.

CONTENTS

Acknowledgments   i

1   Chapter One   7

ACKNOWLEDGMENTS

Thank you to everyone who encouraged me to write. All of your kind words are forever etched in my heart.

To my four daughters (Ny Ny, Ari, Tummy, and ZuZu) I love you more than anything or anyone on this planet. You're the most loving and hardworking girls a woman could ask for. And you are survivors. You deserve a life that provides you the basic things. Along with the balance necessary to continue being great leaders for girls everywhere. I'm so proud of everything that you are; and excited for all that you'll become. And as always... dream bigger. XO

To my parents, Toni and Nathan, who let me be weird; walking around reading all day. I don't think they knew what kinds of books I was reading. (LOL) I thank you. Your tough love, patience and understanding goes a long way; and I had the perfect balance of it all. Thank you! <3

To my brothers, Nate and Mike, I love y'all! Thank you for being good men. Not perfect, but good. You'll make great partners to some lucky women one day ;-)

To my sister, Elita; my best friend... words are not enough. I can't think of all of the times you listened to me say the same thing over and over again. You understand my creative process; and never made me feel like I was annoying you. I'll forever be grateful to you putting up with the most annoying older sister in the world.

And to my best friend since November 1999, my first love... I'll always love you, BB.

To my readers: Your purchase of this book not only helps fund my next project, but $1 of this purchase will be donated to the Sojourner Family Peace Center for all purchases made through June 2018. Their efforts help so many women and children as they transition out of unhealthy living situations. I just want to return some of that love, and bring smiles to the families that are affected by domestic violence.

1 CHAPTER ONE

Shema carefully ejected her zip disk and shut her computer down. Standing up slowly, she stretched long and hard; massaging her temples as she inhaled. When she opened her eyes, she glanced out of the window of her corner office, noticing that most of the cars had cleared the parking structure. A few of the consultants from her marketing company, *Rogers, Inc.* were exiting the building skywalk.

The Las Vegas lights flickered like fireflies in the distance; dancing brighter as the sun disappeared beneath the horizon. Looking down at her watch, the clock changed to 8:30, and she realized she'd reached forty hours of overtime for the third week in a row.

But she wasn't tired. She needed the distraction. Anything to keep her mind from wandering… She had to maintain her sanity.

Shema noticed the missed call icon on her iPhone's home screen.

"*What does he want now,*" she thought; expecting nothing positive to happen should she decide to call him back.

Her ex-husband was calling. Their divorce proceedings finished three months ago and she'd moved the last of her things out of one of their rental properties this past weekend. He'd called multiple times this week, but she refused to answer.

"*I've got to move on.*" Shema thought as she tidied up her desk and put away her files. She uttered these words multiple times daily, but still hadn't fully convinced her heart to let go. She loved her husband with all she knew how, even now. But she finally accepted that love wasn't enough to make their marriage work.

Clicking the light switch in her office, she gathered her coat and purse out of her closet. The glow of the Vegas skyline entered her windows at the perfect angle. She smiled a bittersweet smile, walking through the dark towards the large windows.

This was it… everything she ever wanted.

This was all she ever dreamed about; right up until the day she graduated with her Master's. The day she would finally completed something worth talking about. The day he would be proud of her… because this was what he said he always wanted; for her to live up to her full potential.

The day she found him in the bathroom… fucking one of her classmates like there wasn't a graduation ceremony to attend.

She shook the visual from her head, opening her eyes and unclenching her teeth. She glanced down at her hands, releasing the tight grip she'd placed on the back of her chairs. Why was she even hurt? This wasn't the first time he had cheated.

But it was the first time she'd caught him in the act.

She tried to take his head off that day, managing to snatch her stiletto off and get a few good licks in on him and the quiet bitch from her marketing class, before security hauled her off.

"Get over it, Shema," she said to herself as she walked back towards her door.

Shema pulled the door up behind herself, pulling out her keys. She placed them back in her pocket, checking to make sure her mace was ready, and that her pistol's safety was off.

Just as she turned around, she bumped into Rick so hard, she dropped her keys and purse. The pile of papers he was holding went sliding across the marble tile.

"Dammit, Rick, I told you to leave over an hour ago! You scared the shit out of me!"

"I'm sorry, Ms. Rogers." The vibration of his baritone filled the empty office; the very sound bouncing off of the walls. "Shit, you scared me, too."

No sooner had he uttered the profanity, he stood up, stumbling for an apology. "Ms. Rogers, I'm truly sorry. I didn't mean to use such inappropriate language."

"Shit, damn, motherfucker. We all swear. Just try not to do it when you go to that elementary school next week. Their board of directors may not like that very much."

Rick laughed, his posture relaxing a little. He had a beautiful smile.

"Oh, Rick? Please… call me Shema. You've been here like, six months now, and you still haven't loosened up!"

He chuckled. "Forgive me, Shema. I'm just not used to working for a firm that's so laid back." Shema knew he was telling the truth. He worked for her formal rivals, *Clarkson & Prince*, before joining her team. C&P had a reputation for being the most hard-nosed marketing firm in Vegas.

When news broke about their split, Rick came to *Rogers, Inc.* because he didn't want to work directly under either of the those pricks any longer.

"Why are you still here?"

"No, I left about two hours ago; but I had to come back because I forgot to submit the report to Peter Birmingham for tomorrow's meeting. He's flying in tomorrow afternoon, and I wanted to make sure he had time to look over the documents."

Rick was bending down to get the rest of his papers up. Shema finally noticed that he wasn't wearing the same suit he had on earlier. He'd traded the navy blue tailored suit for gym apparel. She recognized the Adidas jogging pants because Trevor owned a few pairs. But she wasn't sure who made the tank top he was wearing.

What she was sure of? This shirt was giving Shema a very personal view of every muscle on his back. The tag on the back of the shirt said *Jailbodies*. She'd have to look them up online. Maybe they had a female line, too.

Her eyebrow raised at the sight of his arms, watching the tendons and veins work as he shuffled the papers together. Instinctively, she touched her collarbone, suddenly feeling the heat creep up her neck.

It'd been years since she'd even tried to notice anybody but Trevor. But it was hard not to notice Rick.

Shema's mind wandered to the day of his interview. Her former assistant Tami practically ran in her stilettos to inform her that the "chocolate young thunder-cat" in the waiting room was actually her 10:00 AM appointment. Tami liked them young, and sometimes took her harmless flirting too far.

Reminding Tami about the sexual assault case she avoided 2 years earlier, Shema walked towards the escalator, to head down to the waiting area on the ground level floor. As Shema made her journey, she was cut-off by at least seven women, and one guy, trying to peek over the balcony at Rick.

But when he stood up to shake her hand, his broad shoulders, creating a shadow over her, she understood what all of the fuss was about. And when he opened his mouth to say "Nice to meet you," his voice vibrated her root chakras. The icy exterior that Shema had built after her ex's betrayal nearly melted. Purely a physical attraction… she knew nothing about him.

"Are you just going to stand there staring, or are you going to give me a hand?" It was the same voice he was using to cut through her steamy flashback.

"I'm sorry!" Shema blushed; brushing her hair off of her cheek. Her long, natural locks fell into loose curls past her shoulders. She wished she would have worn her usual bun today.

As she bent down to pick up a few papers, she could feel him smiling at her. Damn; he must have caught her looking.

Trying to think of an excuse, Shema blamed her long hours. "I was just… trying to read the tag on your shirt." He looked over at her, eyebrows furrowed. She didn't dare make eye contact. "It's just... I've been putting in so much overtime; I haven't even had time to go to the gym in the last three weeks."

"Oh, really? I would have never guessed." Rick mentally face palmed himself for saying that out loud.

"Umm, thanks? I think..." Shema recognized the compliment, but didn't want to say anything more and risk embarrassing herself any further. Maybe he didn't even notice her eyeballing him.

But Rick *had* noticed, and it was hard to hide his amusement. He'd been working here for over six months. He'd heard the rumors about Shema around the office. Although he typically stayed as far away from office gossip, it was hard not to listen to anything that might help him get ahead with this company.

He'd heard that her husband had cheated on her, and she'd just went through a nasty divorce; so she had been drowning herself in work to avoid going home. He'd also heard how she hadn't gotten laid in about 6 months and that's why she'd been such a hard ass lately.

Rick wasn't stupid... he knew he was an attractive man. He didn't work that hard in the gym to ignore the fact. Blessed with his mother's deep brown skin tone, and his father's height and charcoal eyes; he always turned heads when he entered the room.

But he worked just as hard on his brain as he did his brawn. And at the end of the day, all of his pretty boy looks wouldn't mean shit if he wasn't financially able to hold his own.

So there was no way in hell he was about to throw away his reputation in this field for a spontaneous romp in the hay with the beautiful Shema Rogers.

No matter how fine she was. No matter how much she looked like she needed a shea butter massage from head to toe. Even if her slim waist spread out into the roundest buttocks he'd seen in ages; or if her shirt had unbuttoned and the tops of her caramel colored breasts were fully exposed to a large, brown nipple while she helped him gather the papers she'd knocked out of his hand.

No sooner had he took in the beautiful sight, he felt his dick begin to swell. "*Down, boy... you're not in high school anymore,*" he told himself.

Rick quickly turned around, acting as if he were engrossed in organizing the stack. Maybe if he gave her a few minutes, she'd figure out she was compromised.

"I think that's everything." Shema stood up to hand Rick the papers. Oblivious to the fact that her breast was still visible, she blew her curls out of her face. Shema noticed that Rick wasn't really working, but he hadn't stood up yet.

"Rick!"

Rick stood up abruptly, and faced her slowly. Just as he thought... her tittie was still hanging out. And it was hanging out even more now because her shirt was completely unbuttoned. The other one had now peeked its head out to join the party.

"Umm... Ms. Rogers?" He was looking above her head.

"Shema, Rick. What am I going to do with you? It's not such a big deal to be on a first name basis, you know?" She blew her hair curls out of her face again, the annoyance making her look that much more adorable. He reached up and pulled her hair out of her face, tucking it behind her ear.

Embarrassed, because she was never this frazzled, she adjusted the stack of folders. "Uh... thanks?"

"You're welcome." Rick couldn't help but smile. He was amused at how nervous she was around him. She was normally in control of her surroundings. His ego made him think that she was only this nervous because of him.

Rick suddenly had the bright idea to extend this awkward exchange even longer. He glanced down again. He felt like such a pervert, taking advantage of her ignorance of her current state. But she was beautiful, her breasts shimmering in the dimmed office lighting. He would've been happy just looking a little longer. He wondered if anyone else knew she had piercings...

Shema was still holding onto the stack of papers. Her arms were extended from the weight of the files. The position of her arms was now giving her cleavage an unnecessary boost.

She looked at him in annoyance. Why hadn't he taken the files from her? His hands weren't even that full.

"Rick... do you mind taking these from me?"

Rick decided enough was enough. "Um, sure Shema. But first, do you mind if I help you out with something else?"

"What, is my hair coming back down?"

Rick smirked as he reached towards her blouse and closed her shirt.

"What are you..." Shema followed his hand, her eyes bucked in horror as she caught both of her nipple piercings as he covered her up.

"OH MY GOD!" Shema dropped the files on the floor again, and took off running towards her door.

Rick couldn't help but laugh, but he kept the sound down. He expected her to be embarrassed. He waited a few seconds, and then walked after her just as she got her door unlocked and ran into her office. She tried to shut the door behind herself, but she somehow dropped her purse, and it was blocking the way. He peeked into her office, she was nowhere in sight.

"Shema?" He called her name.

"GO AWAY, RICK!" Shema fought hard to keep her voice from shaking.

Was she crying? Oh, shit. He felt like an ass.

"Shema… it's not a big deal!" He stepped into the dark office, the moonlight shining onto her desk; the lights of the Las Vegas Skyline dancing in the distance. "I barely even saw anything, the lights were dim!"

"Yeah right!" She reached inside of her blazer pocket for a tissue.

"Fuck it," she thought, using her sleeve.

"Where are you?" He was all the way in the office now, but she was nowhere in sight. He didn't want to enter too far. She was still his boss.

What the hell was he thinking? Now this scenario could only go one of two ways: He could calm her down, and keep his job; or not calm her down, and she'd fire him. And probably file a sexual harassment claim.

"Shema, I'm sorry. I tried to say something, but I didn't want you to be embarrassed." He took another step in. *Where was she?* "Shema?" He got closer to the window. Her desk was right in front of the glass.

"I'm right here."

Rick looked down, his eyes widened as he saw her feet sticking out from under her desk. Now he really felt like an ass. He hadn't even taken into consideration the emotional state she was in. He wasn't thinking of her divorce, or the fact that she'd been single for a few months now. He didn't know her sex life, but from the looks of it; she hasn't been with anyone or she wouldn't be this nervous. He didn't take pride in making women cry.

As Rick stood in front of the desk, Shema sat under the table, looking out at his legs, her eyes lifted up, only able to see his mid-thigh and…

Oh shit!

Shema didn't know how it happened, but the tip of Rick's penis met her gaze. It had somehow fallen out of the bottom of his shorts. It was blacker than he was; the one eyed monster staring at her under the desk.

"Oh my God…"

"Shema, I told you, I barely saw anything!" Rick had no clue his johnson was as free as a bird.

"This is crazy!" Shema had her hands on her head in disbelief. He couldn't see her.

"I know, you should just come out from under the desk. It's just a breast. I've seen thousands."

"No, I mean, YOU!" She reached out from under the desk and pointed to his dick head with a perfectly manicured nail.

"WHAT THE HELL?!" Rick turned around quickly, trying to tuck his dick back into his shorts. He should have worn his other tights. He wasn't expecting all of this commotion.

Shema just sat under the desk. She was almost on the verge of another panic attack before Rick's… slip up.

Now… she looked out into the night sky, and thought about all of the things that led her to this point. She'd never slept with another man before or after Trevor. She had a weak moment a month after the graduation incident and called him up. But by the time he came to her apartment, she had talked some sense into The very thought of being intimate, or baring herself to anyone else actually scared her. It was probably the reason she stayed in that sorry excuse of a marriage for as long as she did.

It was stupid, she knew that much. But somewhere inside, she still believed in the fairytale. But here she was, flashing tits and balls with her assistant.

No sooner had the thought entered her mind, she burst into laughter. Rick had been pacing around the room trying to think of a logical explanation for why his junk had fallen out of his shorts. He was large, so it happened all of the time, which is why he wore his sport tights underneath his gym attire during cardio.

But why was she laughing? He was a little unnerved by the sound. It's not the reaction most women gave when they were blessed to see The Beast.

He walked over to the desk again, and slowly kneeled down. He met her amused gaze with one of confusion. "*What the hell,*" he thought. "*Might as well just be myself. This shit can't get any worse.*"

"So... how about those piercings, Ms. Rogers?" He smiled.

"Rick..."

"What?!" he laughed. "You've seen my dick; I've seen your piercings. We're about as out there as two people can be."

She laughed again. This could not be happening. She was not sitting around discussing her nipple piercings with him like it was a casual conversation.

"You keep laughing. I'm not sure if I should be bothered or not."

"What? Why should you be bothered?"

"Well... my junk fell out; then you laughed." Shema looked confused, then her eyes opened wide.

"No! I wasn't laughing about that! I would never... I mean... never mind." She tried to read the look on his face.

"Oh, I knew you weren't laughing at the size." His tone was defensive, but Shema didn't know why. It was obvious he was packing.

"So what is it, hmm? Are you just used to women jumping all over you, throwing their panties at you when you walk by?"

"Well... yeah; sort of!" Rick said this proudly, which caused Shema to laugh a little bit more. "I'm just saying... you could have done anything. But you laughed."

"Are you mad... or *naw?*" Shema tilted her head, her curls falling to one side of her face.

"Really, Shema?" He looked at her under the desk, her sarcastic expression too cute for him to stay mad, and they both burst into laughter. Rick was caught off guard, realizing that he had never heard her laugh... or had even seen her smile much since he'd started working here. From the little tidbits he'd heard around the office, her husband cheated on her the day of her graduation, she beat his ass, the girl's ass, and two of the security guards who were breaking up the altercation were hurt in the process. She was still going through court proceedings to pay for the damages she'd caused.

"Note to self... don't piss her off." he thought.

But looking at her, she was anything but violent. She was beautiful... and surprisingly, pretty damn funny. She stayed in her office most of the time working. When she did come out, it was to check on client's files and make sure that all of her employees had what they needed in order to close the deals. She truly cared about everyone around her.

"Can you please come out from under the desk?"

Shema looked at him, wanting to trust that he simply wanted to help. It wasn't that she didn't trust him… she didn't trust her next move. She was truly confused and more vulnerable than she'd been in a while. And this entire evening was more excitement than she'd had in months.

Rick smiled at her, and proceeded to melt the core of her defenses with one word:

"Please?"

Shema handed him her hand, and he gently pulled her from under the desk. As she stood up, she instinctively reached for her shirt. She'd tried fastening the shirt while she was under the desk, but she'd missed a lot of buttons. As she attempted to fix the shirt again, she realized he was less than a foot away from her. His closeness made her breathing ragged, and she was missing buttons all over again. Rick chuckled softly, causing Shema to turn away defensively.

"Now you're laughing at me."

"No! It's just that I don't know why you're so embarrassed."

"This isn't me. I'm not easily frazzled." Her hands and voice were shaking, and she kept missing the hole in her shirt. "Shit! I don't even know why this shirt came unbuttoned; I just bought it last month."

"Well, you said it's been a month since you've been in the gym; so maybe…"

Shema whipped back around and faced him; annoyed. "Maybe; *what?!*" She placed her hands on her hips, the motion causing her top buttons to open up again.

Rick couldn't hold his laughter any longer. He sat on her desk, his hearty laugh bouncing off of the walls. Shema dropped her head in defeat. What the hell was happening?

"Can I help? You honestly look like you need some help."

"No! I don't need help buttoning a fucking shirt."

Rick knew she wasn't really upset, plus he was too amused to let her ruin this moment for him. He reached out, grabbed her by the waist, and pulled her close. If she was going to fire him after this entire ordeal, at least he'd have a memory to hold onto.

Shema gasped in disbelief. Who the hell did he think he was?! Just as she prepared for him to try to steal a kiss or cop a feel… he began to button her shirt.

He was sitting on her desk, and he was still taller than Shema. She looked up at him with the most confused face; contemplating pushing him away, but her mixed emotions wouldn't let her. Plus, he was staring right through her.

"Why are you so angry?"

"I'm not… I'm just frustrated."

"Why? Have I done something to you?" He buttoned another button, the whole while looking her in the eye. He studied her every expression; watching her squirm. She reached up to move his hands, but he gently pushed her hands out of the way.

"No, you haven't done anything! I'm your boss! This is just highly inappropriate! What if someone were to walk up and see us? I'd never be able to explain what really happened."

"Who cares? You're the boss. Plus, word around the office is you could use a little distraction."

"What the hell…?!" Shema firmly grabbed his hands and pushed them away. She stepped back, bumping into the window behind her. "What do you mean 'word around the office'?"

"I mean… people are saying you could use a little… relaxing… to make things a little less frigid around here."

Shema had heard enough. How *dare* he or *anyone* imply anything about her personal life? "Mr. Perkins, where the hell do you get off…"

"Hold on, Shema; I just started working here what, six months ago? How the hell would I know anything about the office or anything unless someone else was discussing it? It's not like I went around gossiping like a little…" Rick caught himself before he took the conversation too far. "I apologize. I don't want to offend you. I just figured instead of listening to everyone discuss you like they knew your story, I'd ask you for myself."

Shema was angry. She had no idea she'd developed a reputation around the office. She'd always prided herself on providing her employees with a warm and inviting work environment. She kept an open door policy.

Well… she used to.

"I don't know what to say, Rick."

"You don't have to say anything. I'm not one to judge. My divorce was 3 years ago. This single shit is not cool."

Shema turned and looked at him. What was his story? Did he cheat on his wife, too? From his pretty boy looks and smooth demeanor, she figured that had to be the case.

"So what, did you cheat so many times, she finally decided enough was enough?"

"What?" Rick had been looking out at the beautiful skyline. Her words caused him to turn around. "What did you say?"

"I just asked how many times did you cheat on your wife before she finally called it quits?"

Shema was sitting on the sofa in her office, adjusting her shirt again. She didn't even see him walk towards her. Suddenly, his large shadow blocked her view of her top, and she glanced up in time to see him crouch down before her.

Rick kept calm, but his annoyance slowly surfaced.

"I would never cheat on my wife. But she left me for a diplomat in Ghana. The title of 'First Lady' was more appealing than 'Mrs. Rick Perkins,' so she walked." He looked at Shema with a blank stare. "What; are you always this judgmental? Is that why your husband cheated on you?"

Shema smacked him before her brain had time to stop her.

"Oh yeah, I heard you like to fight, too. Is this what he had to look forward to everyday when he came home?"

Shema smacked him again. He looked at her, his dark eyes emotionless; his chiseled features glowing against the moonlight. She swung again, but he caught her wrist mid-swing. Shema let go of her shirt and started swinging at him so fast, he fell back from his crouching position while trying to dodge her blows.

Her hits didn't hurt. He'd lost his balance, and landed on his butt. She jumped off of the couch and landed on top of him, straddling his muscular thighs. She raised her hand again, but stopped when she saw him staring through her.

Rick didn't even attempt to block her hits anymore. She didn't know why.

Shema climbed off of him, confused as hell, and angrier than a menstruating grizzly bear. But she wasn't mad at him. She was mad at herself, mad at Trevor, mad at everything lately…

"Rick… I'm so sorry! This isn't me. I don't know what's happening to me." She looked out of the window, the moonlight shining brighter than before.

"Is this what you need?" His voice calm as he sat up; Rick decided to call her bluff. He knew she wasn't crazy. But a broken heart can make some people lose it. "Is this going to make you feel better? Then hit me. I can take it."

"No, I don't want to hit you, Rick…"

"Go ahead… hit me, Shema. Because you really want to hit him, don't you?" He crawled slid towards her; as she slid backwards, falling against the window. "You're mad, right?"

Closing her eyes, she shook her head no. She felt herself shaking; the emotions building up inside. "Come on, Shema." She covered ears. He leaned in closer, and raising his voice a little louder, he exclaimed: "Hit me!" "What's wrong with you!?!" Shema screamed. She tried to stand up, falling back on her butt against the windowpane. "Stop it! I'm not angry!"

"Then what is it, huh? What are you feeling *right now*?" He moved in closer watching her body tense up. "What do you feel, Shema?"

Shema had been mad for so long… this night with Rick was the first time she felt something other than mad. With Rick, she felt excitement, confusion, and embarrassment. Shema felt vulnerable… but still felt strong. Physically, he could take whatever he wanted from her without asking. His large frame towered over hers, but he didn't intimidate her. In fact; Shema felt like she controlled this entire exchange, even though she was the one with her back against the glass.

"Rick please; I don't want to hit you. I don't know why I hit you. I'm sorry. I'm not crazy."

"I know you're not, Shema." He backed away from her slightly, "All black men don't cheat. Just like I know all black women aren't crazy." He watched her facial expressions soften, tears filling her eyes.

Shema slumped back onto the floor. Quietly she cried, tears streaming down her neck. She felt the warm tears on the tops of her breasts, realizing she still hadn't fixed her damn shirt.

"What do you feel, Shema?"

"I don't know what I'm feeling, Rick!" Shema wiped her face unsuccessfully, the tears falling faster than her hands could get rid of them. Rick looked up and saw a Kleenex box on her desk. Standing up and adjusting his clothes, he walked over to grab the box, only to find it empty inside. He looked over at her and wondered how many other days she'd spent crying in this office.

Before he realized it, he'd pulled his shirt off. Easing himself onto the floor next to her, he studied her face. She was beautiful, but the shadows of exhaustion were etched over her golden features. Rick handed her his shirt.

Shema didn't look up to see what he had handed her. She felt something soft touch her arm, and assuming it was a handkerchief, she accepted. As she wiped the tears from her face, she inhaled, and froze. The smell of deodorant, a hint of male body wash, and what she now recognized as his natural scent; filled her nostrils.

She opened her eyes; focusing on the *Jailbodies* tag she observed earlier. She touched the tag, more aware of the knowledge that if she held this shirt, he was sitting next to her, half naked... in all of his big black glory.

Shema didn't dare look up. Not because of what she thought he'd do to her… but what she'd do to him.

She couldn't explain it, but she felt safe with him.

If he were trying to take advantage of her, he could have by now. He knew she was weak.

And that's why Rick didn't take advantage. When his wife first left, he was hurting. He was hurting so bad, he was determined to return that pain to any woman he encountered.

But it truly wasn't who he was. And the more women he used, the emptier he felt. He'd taken an unofficial vow of celibacy; giving himself time to *feel* again…That was six months ago; when he first started working at *Rogers, Inc.*

This was before he met the beautiful Shema Rogers in person. The attraction had always been strong between them; from the moment he stood up in the high rise lobby to shake her hand before the interview; until this very moment. There was no denying the sensation he felt whenever she walked past. And as confident as she seemed in the boardroom, she became almost shy whenever he was near.

Almost as shy as she looked right now.

Unable to resist the urge any longer, Rick reached over and cupped her chin; gently lifting her tear stained face. Since she had long stopped wiping the tears, he took the shirt back from her.

Then he began slowly wiping her face for her.

Shema tried not to think. She closed her eyes, basking in the warmth of physical touch, allowing him to clean her up. Rick first wiped her cheeks, once again removing the curl from the front of her face… before reaching behind her head and removing the clip that held her hair.

As her curls fell, Shema looked up at him, confused. "Why did you do that?"

"It seems like your curls wanted to be free. I wanted to set… you… free."

Shema looked into his eyes, the same eyes that looked through her so many times before. She studied his entire face. He was truly handsome. His jaw bone was strong; she could see him clenching his face muscles. What she didn't know was Rick was biting the inside of his cheek to keep from kissing her at that very moment.

Rick slowly wiped the tear streaks that had slid down her neck. As his eyes roamed lower, he could see her breathing quicken, causing her breasts to rise and fall a little faster than before. He wiped the tears that had slid down between her cleavage.

As Shema closed her eyes again, she instinctively rolled her head back, allowing the fabric to soak up the liquid. She was beginning to sweat. She'd almost forgotten what it felt like to be wanted…

Almost sensing her thoughts, Rick leaned forward, kissing the tears as they mixed with the sweat beads that had built up along her collarbone.

Shema shuddered at the feel of his warm mouth along her neck, welcoming the sensation. She exhaled softly, deciding at that moment to… feel.

In one swift motion, Rick picked her up off of the floor; holding her in the air until she opened her legs on both sides of him. He lowered her down onto his lap; sitting up just enough to place his lips on hers.

Although Shema could sense this moment was coming, she wasn't prepared for the warmth that filled her when their lips finally touched.

Rick reached up to touch her chin, his thumb trailing along the soft skin of her bottom lip. So many times he'd looked at her beautiful mouth. It was only right that he explored it first. He was pleased to find that she opted for a strawberry flavored lip balm. The taste mixed well with her salty tears.

Shema was resisting; but Rick was patient. As he teased her lips with his tongue, her lips finally parted; giving him freedom to taste her. Surprisingly, she slipped her tongue into his mouth, putting her arms around his neck.

Shema didn't know what was happening to her. She felt… hungry. She needed to feel him in every way. She kissed him deeply, biting his lip harder than she'd realized.

"Shit…"

"I'm sorry… I wasn't trying to bite you." Shema reached up to touch his lip.

Rick leaned back, to see her face. This was the most peaceful he'd ever seen her. He reached both hands around her ass, pulling her in closer. She moaned into his mouth, her breath sweet and warm. Rick's manhood swelled uncontrollably, but he fought the urge to release The Beast.

Instead, Rick stood up. As her legs dropped to the ground, their lips parted. She looked up into his eyes as he stood up.

"What do you want from me?"

Shema understood the question; she just didn't want to sound stupid trying to answer.

"What do you want from me, Shema? I don't expect anything from you right now. But I can tell you need something from me. What is it?"

"I… don't know." Her eyes dropped to the floor, and she began fiddling with her hair again.

Rick took her chin and lifted her head. "Don't do that."

"Do what?"

"Drop your head when I speak to you. You have no reason to be nervous around me. I won't judge you."

"But… it's just that…"

"What; we work together? You're my boss? Don't worry; I won't ever speak of this moment if you don't want me to. I don't snitch on my dick."

Shema felt the heat rising. She had never talked so candidly about sex with anyone but her husband before now.

"No, it's not that. It's just that I've *only* been with Trevor... sexually." Rick looked at her, as she looked away. He was amused, but didn't want to laugh and throw her off.

"So, that's it? That's all you're worried about?" He lifted her up to meet his gaze. "What else?"

"I'm just afraid that I'll look stupid... inexperienced."

"Shema... you're too beautiful to ever look stupid." He leaned forward to place kisses on her neck. The confidence that made her a beast in the board room was faltering. He was trying to remain calm, but her nervousness made her look slightly vulnerable... making his dick even harder. "Do you trust me?"

Shema opened her eyes, confused. "How can I trust you if we're not even... dating... or..."

"We don't have to be dating in order for you to trust the kind of man that I've shown you on a daily basis. I work for you. I'm your right hand man. Do you trust me?"

She closed her eyes, trying to say the word 'yes' but her lips wouldn't move.

Rick turned and sat her on her desk and began to unbutton her blouse, moving her hands as she tried to slow him down. "Do you trust me?" She didn't respond, so he ripped the rest of her buttons, and tossed her shirt.

"Why did you do that?!"

"You were taking too long. Do you trust me?" He reached down and removed her shoes one by one.

"Rick, I'm just trying to get my thoughts together." Shema was stalling the inevitable. Everything within her was telling her to stop; but the ache Rick was creating between her thighs kept her planted in one spot.

"Still stalling?" Rick slid his hands up, gripped her thighs, and ripped her pantyhose. As he tossed them aside, he chuckled at all of the cuss words Shema was spewing.

"I'll buy you some more. Do you trust me?" He reached up for the zipper on her skirt.

Shema loved this skirt too much to let him rip it off. To his obvious amusement, she reached around and unzipped the skirt herself. She cursed again.

"Thank you." Rick smiled as he removed the skirt. Her thick thighs and ass spread on the desk. He leaned down and kissed the crease of her hips, slowly parting her thighs, planting kisses all the way down to the insides of her knees. She was still resisting, but not for long.

As he stood up, he took in the view of her bronze colored skin in the burgundy colored lingerie set. The cream lace that lined the top of her panties was in the shape of a "v" and followed the shape of her curves.

"You're beautiful... even more than I could have imagined."

"Thank you." Shema shivered as she felt his gaze.

"Shema... do you trust me? He began to unbutton her bra. She protectively reached up, crossing her arms in an attempt to not let her bra drop.

"Rick... I want to trust you. This is crazy." He slid her bra down over each breast, laughing as she hurried to keep him from viewing.

"You know I've already seen your breast 3 times tonight..."

"Shit." Shema slowly lowered her arms.

Leaning down, he grabbed her ankles. Sliding his hands up her legs, he stopped when he got to her panties. He looked her in her eyes as he began sliding them off.

Shema thought about stopping him, but realized how foolish she must already look. She looked at his muscular arms, as he effortlessly lifted her hips and slid her panties down over her knees. Her desk felt cold against her bottom.

Rick kneeled down between her legs. She was manicured, which was good for him. But she left just enough of the dark curls to let him know she was a grown ass woman. He could smell her, even from here. Her natural scent was complemented by whatever she used. It couldn't have been perfume... he was allergic.

"What is this scent you use?" He leaned closer to her vagina, taking in the scent.

"It's a body oil... I'm allergic to sprays." She shivered, practically dying at the thought that he was this close to...her.

Rick laughed. "I'm allergic, too." While he was talking, he parted her legs, exposing her beautiful fruit. She was moist; her juices were glistening against the Las Vegas lights. The thought of tasting her was running through his mind, but he knew it'd be too much for her to bear.

He'd had enough. He didn't want to scare her, but he needed to explore her... now.

Shema watched with anxious arousal as Rick kneeled before her. He had been massaging her feet the entire time. Again, he inhaled her fragrance, getting closer to her throbbing honeypot. He got within an inch of her fruit, close enough for the heat of his words to surround her.

"Do you *want* to trust me?"

Shema closed her eyes, her head falling backwards as she rested on her elbows. His warm breath nearly penetrated her to the core. He was waiting on her to give the okay. If she said no, she'd regret it more than she would if she walked away.

"Yes, I want..."

Before she could finish the words, Rick cupped her buttocks, lifting her yoni into his mouth.

Shema gasped, more from shock than anything else. Covering her mouth with one hand, she tried to sit up on the other arm; but Rick's hand slid up to her chest, his muscular arm holding her at bay.

Her breathing quickened, as she watched him work. His mouth was warm as his tongue slowly tasted her sweetness.

Rick knew she'd taste sweet. He knew when he first kneeled in front of her nicely manicured puss. He prayed she wouldn't say "no," because he would have walked away like a man, but been as mad as a kid denied ice cream on a warm day.

"Rick, wait!" Shema panted between breaths. Rick stopped. "Wait… wha…why did you stop."

"Because you asked me to." Rick hid his amusement. She was cute when she was confused.

"But I didn't really mean 'stop' stop…"

"Then tell me what to do. In order for this to work, I need to obey your every command, I need you to trust me."

Shema stared at him, realizing the game. She controlled this exchange. She'd never felt this sort of power before… she liked it.

"Go."

Rick smirked, and lowered his head. They didn't break eye contact, the expression on Shema's face one of ecstasy and amusement. She finally let go of every inhibition, her head falling back.

Shema felt the wave of a powerful orgasm coming. Her eyes wide as she stared at the ceiling, she reached down and grabbed the back of Rick's head. She started to squeeze her legs together, but Rick pulled them back apart. She looked at him like he was crazy, about to scream 'wait'… realizing she didn't want him to. She wanted was about to happen.

When she felt his finger slip into her wetness to tickle her g-spot, his mouth still actively suckling her pearl; she released everything within.

"Oh GOD!" She cried out, every inhibition gone. She didn't care who was in the building. Nothing was going to take this moment from her.

That's all Rick was waiting on. He stood up, her fruit still in his mouth; now her essence glistening on his beard. Wrapping his hands under her back, he hijacked her svelte frame in the air.

"What are you doing?!" She looked down at him, his face still between her legs.

Rick didn't say a word. He knew she would protest. He walked over towards the window. As soon as she saw his intent, she pulled his ears.

"No!"

"Okay." He stood there, looking up at her, waiting for her instruction. He was pretty strong, but he was thankful that she wasn't too heavy. He could stand there all day. "What now?"

This was too much for Shema to grasp. She knew what he was getting ready to do. But she was afraid.

"What if someone sees us up here? What if they recognize us?"

Rick laughed, knowing she would say that. "Shema... we're on the top floor, and we're facing the parking structure. And everyone is gone." He saw her turn around, as if verifying his words. "You can see out, but no one can see you."

Shema looked out at the night sky. The lights from the strip weren't too far away. She knew he was right. No one could possibly see them.

Shema looked down at his handsome face. Damn, he was fine. For the first time, since their exchange began, she felt comfortable. So much so... she smiled.

Caught off guard at the glow that crossed her face, Rick smiled back.

"You're really strong."

"Thank you." Rick kissed her wetness. Shema shuddered, grabbing his head. Rick laughed. "You wanna know what I was going to do?" He kissed her again, causing her to gasp. "Is that a yes?"

Shema opened her eyes, looked down at his face, the moon glistening off of his beautiful skin. Biting her lip, she nodded.

Rick walked over to the window, planting more kisses on her kitty. As soon as he reached the window, he gently pressed Shema's back against the pane. He spread her legs wide, and intensely dined on her. She moaned loudly, trying to squeeze her legs together. He pressed both thighs back against the glass. Thankful that she was flexible, he could stay in the position for hours. She felt so good in his hands.

Shema was moaning so intensely, she didn't even recognize her own sounds. She opened her eyes, turning her head and looking down at the parking structure. The lights flickered so brightly, she suddenly became fully aware of where she was. He suckled harder. She needed to say something... she needed to think...

"Rick... do you... think... someone will... recognize... recognize..." She stuttered between breaths,

He spoke to her, never breaking contact with her pearl. "No one is going to recognize you in this position." He kissed her again.

Rick lowered her down, enjoying her silky skin as she slid down his body. When he came face to face with her, he paused.

"Do you want me?" He lifted her up, inserting his middle and ring finger into her juices. He watched her eyes close as her head rolled back.

Shema was panting; the soft but firm strokes of his finger were driving her to madness. She knew what he was asking... just like she knew he was holding back. She knew once she said yes, he would give her all that he'd been restraining.

"Tasting you was more than enough..." Rick's husky, tone emitted the obvious passion he was holding back. The vibration of his voice; and the frequency of his sound shook Shema to her very core.

"Shema... I need more of you now... But I won't move from this spot until you say..."

"Yes."

Rick set Shema on her feet and untied his shorts. He grabbed the large office chair and her hand, headed towards the desk. He lifted her onto her desk. The bulge in his shorts was slowly moving up, the fabric of his shorts were doing a poor job of providing privacy. Finally he pulled the drawstring, his shorts falling slowly, revealing his fully erect package.

Shema's eyes widened. The preview she had earlier was nothing in comparison to the beautiful specimen that stood before her now. As she noticed his member was naturally shifted to the side, she looked into his eyes with a coy smile. Not to her surprise, he smiled back, releasing He removed his shirt; his dark skin flexing and glowing with the flicker of the Las Vegas lights. His body was amazing; crafted by his vegan lifestyle.

Rick watched her face as her eyes scanned his body. Her approval was appreciated. He got ready to remove his socks, but Shema stood and said

"Let me."

"Wait... What?" Rick was slightly confused.

"You removed everything else before I could help. Plus... I like feet." Rick laughed before he could catch himself. "What, you got some kind of foot fetish or something?"

Shema laughed and dropped down to remove his socks. Face to face with his erect cock, Shema stopped. She looked at it... The beautiful specimen was slightly curved to the left. He wasn't even fully erect, but his impressive size caused her vagina to jolt.

Rick looked down at her, watching her facial expression. His dick hardened at the thought of her lips wrapped around him. He wondered if she was experienced, or if he'd have fun teaching her how to pleasure him. But he didn't want it. Not this time. He needed to feel her love wrapped around him. His throbbing manhood wanted to feel a different kind of warmth... the one that could only be satisfied once it was surrounded by the slick essence of a yoni.

Shema couldn't believe she was contemplating tasting him... right there. He'd licked her so good earlier, she felt like returning the favor. But she'd only given oral to her husband. The thought of freely giving it to another man had never crossed her mind until now.

She knew she would please him; she enjoyed giving head more than she would ever admit. And right now... she almost *needed* to taste him.

Just as she looked up at him, preparing to take him in, Rick gently cupped her chin.

"Not this time." He smiled at the brief moment of disappointment that crossed her face. *"Next time,"* he thought as he lifted her up onto her desk.

Shema suddenly stopped, looking Rick in the face, before dropping her eyes. "Do you have a condom?" *"Please say 'yes'..."* she thought. She didn't want to choose her right mind this time.

He walked over to his duffle bag, but turned around to face her.

"Don't say anything crazy."

Shema laughed. "What? Why would I?"

He pulled out a STILL-wrapped 12 pack of Magnum XL's. Shema tried to stifle her laugh, but it escaped through her fingers.

"What."

"So... are you just extra prepared for romps like this or... what?"

Rick started opening the box, irritated with the tight seal. "No, actually... I bought these about 7 months ago. But... never got a chance to use them."

Shema was headed towards him with a pair of scissors, but she stopped at his admission.

"Wait... you haven't... in seven months?" Rick looked up at her, a little annoyed at her obvious humor over his drought.

Shema laughed... heartily. And as much as Rick wanted to be annoyed... he actually stopped, realizing it was the first time he'd heard her laugh so loudly. Her breast rose and fell with each breath, and then she snorted; cute as hell.

Rick chuckled. "What the hell is so funny, woman?"

Shema coughed as she passed him the scissors. "I'm sorry... I'm not judging you. It's just... why? It's obvious that physically... you fit the stereotype."

Rick got the box opened, and snatched off a little gold packet, and looked into her eyes. And for a moment he almost trusted her enough to tell her a part of his past. But there was no need. He walked up to her and kissed her on the forehead. "I don't know; I was just dealing with a lot of shit. Didn't feel like it."

Shema closed her eyes. She knew the feeling. Sixteen months since the graduation incident... she hasn't even thought about sex. But then again... she couldn't remember the last time she felt like... this. Sexy... desirable... wanted.

Rick leaned down to kiss her lips. Her head rolled back, as he left a trail of kisses along her jawbone.

"Rick..." Shema moaned; basking in the glow of the moonlight. His kiss deepened as he turned her back toward the chaise lounge, and lowered her body down. He cuffed her peach with his right hand.

"I'm going to take it as slow as you want... But I'm going to enjoy this, too. And when I know you're ready... I'm taking over." The huskiness of his voice was intense.

Their eyes locked as he lifted her slightly, positioning himself to enter her warmth. Her expression was calm as she anticipated his penetration, but inside she was vibrating, her senses fully aware of what her body was about to receive.

His first thrust was controlled. As her lips parted, making way for a small breath to escape, he paused and allowed her to take in what he had given her. He had more to go, and he needed her to enjoy it once it was time to give her the rest.

He was thick, Shema observed, which was a good thing, because she didn't want to spend her time comparing him to her ex.

"You okay?" Shema was confused as she nodded. *"It's not like I'm a virgin."*

His second stroke was deeper. Shema's eyes widened, looking up into his face.

"Rick, wait… let me…"

The third stroke was the deepest… powerful. She gasped loudly, waiting for the next wave.

Rick lifted her up, sliding in and out of her folds. Each thrust felt better than the last. She hugged him perfectly; her tight puss gripping his thickness with each stroke.

He hadn't been inside of her long. Her eyes rolled back, the sudden sounds of her gasps filling the office. When her juices rolled down his balls, Rick was caught off guard by the heat of her sliding down his leg.

Shema ignored him. Her first orgasm without a vibrator in over a year, she knew she'd come hard. She just didn't expect to be so loud. But she didn't care.

Rick began stroking again. Walking backwards towards the couch, he enjoyed watching her abandon all of her perfectionist demeanor. Her body was beautifully sculpted. As he sat down, she straddled his muscular thighs, and began to ride him.

Shema took it all in… every inch. That first orgasm was good. But now that she was up top, she had control of it all. She hadn't enjoyed sex like this since she found out about all of the other women her ex had fucked during their marriage.

"What are you thinking about?"

Shema paused, heat rising to her face. "Why; did I do something wrong?"

"No… you sort of left for a moment… like something had crossed your mind." When she didn't respond, he sat up and looked her in the eyes. Grabbing her hips, he pulled her forward, allowing all of his length to go inside. She gasped loudly; her cries filling the large office. Then suddenly, he began to rock her slowly.

"Shema… we're here; in this moment. Whatever you're thinking, if it causes you not to enjoy this moment, forget it. I'm here for your pleasure right now."

Shema's head rolled back, as she listened to his words. His calm voice a direct contradiction to the beating he was putting on her vagina. Her arms around his neck, she rode him like a pro.

He was larger than she had anticipated. As she came the second time, she gripped him until the wave passed, and releasing her grip as her juices flowed into his lap.

"Damn, Shema...you're going to fuck this couch up." He tried to stay in control when she began rising up and down on top of him. The look on her face let him know she was just getting started. "Shema, I'm trying not to come. But it's been awhile for me, too."

Shema suddenly turned around, facing the room like he was. Her body felt hot; every nerve on edge. She could feel the muscles in his thighs as she used them for leverage.

She positioned her legs on the ground, stood up, and then came down smoothly on his dick. She flipped her damp hair over her shoulder, and looked back at him. The look on her face pure pleasure as she closed her eyes, and restarted the ride.

Rick sat up, reaching up to cup both of her breasts as she continued rising up and down. Her beauty was so different now that her confidence had come out. He felt her wetness surrounding him; but when he looked down and saw the puddle of creamy white gathered at the base of his cock, he leaned back, and closed his eyes.

"Damn, girl!" His voice was scratchy, full of pure ecstasy. "You're riding the hell out of this… shit!"

Shema could have gone on forever. He was so hard. The unmistakable sound of passion in his voice was turning her on.

Rick suddenly grabbed her ass and slowed her down. He was lying back against the couch, but sat up and suddenly lifted her off of him. He stood up, and wrapped his arm around her, pulling her close for a sudden kiss.

He wasn't ready to come yet, but she was doing everything in her power to make him bust.

Her lips were pliant; he controlled them with every slow, deliberate flick of his tongue. As she moaned his name into his mouth, Rick wrapped his other arm around her. Lifting her up, he walked towards the window. When he got to the glass, he gently pressed her back against one of the large panes.

The sudden cool against her skin was relief from the heat that was radiating from their bodies. When he slid back inside, Shema opened her eyes and looked into his. They were a beautiful shade of brown. He was quite handsome; his beard still glistening from snacking on her earlier.

She closed her eyes, and rocked with the motion. He was holding her up at eye level. It wasn't until she saw the city lights reflecting in his pupils, that she realized she was against the window of her office completely naked.

"RICK!" She cried out in surprise, and wrapped her legs around him tightly. Reality set in, and another orgasm began. "Rick… we have to move… OH!"

Rick knew what she would say. "Do you really want me to move?" He let her finish her orgasm, and then stood her on her own two feet. Her damp curls clinging to her face, Rick turned her to face the window.

Before she could protest, he firmly thrust into her. He didn't move. He leaned forward; his warm breath filled her ear. "Do you want to move? He licked the sweat off of her neck, leaving a soft kiss behind her ear.

Shema moaned. "No… don't stop." Rick began stroking again. "Don't stop, Rick…" She repeated the demand, her bare breasts pressed against the glass.

Her voice in his ear, Rick reached around to stimulate her clitoris. Shema's gasps filled the room. He wasn't sure how long they had gone, but he knew he was about to release. He wrapped his other hand around her waist, and pulled her closer to him as he thrust a few more times.

Shema felt him coming to a climax. She was sprawled against the window, looking out at the city lights as her last wave passed.

Rick's breath was ragged as he collapsed against the window. He was still inside of her. Could it have been the fact that he hadn't had sex in a while? Or was it possible that he hadn't enjoyed sex like this in a while?

He looked down on top of her head. Leaning down, he noticed her eyes were closed. The sweat glistened on her brow and top lip. He kissed her on the forehead.

"Are you okay?" He tilted her face towards his. He needed to look into her eyes. She opened them up. A slow smile crossed her face as she leaned up and kissed him softly on the lips.

He reluctantly pulled out of her warmth as she turned around to face him. Shema slipped her arms around his neck, looking him right in the eyes.

"Yes. I'm fine. I'm good." Her golden brown cheeks looked flushed. He pushed her hair out of her eyes, smiling at the soft look on her face.

"Are you sure?" Rick needed a second if she wanted a round two. In all honesty, she wore him out. But he would gladly go again.

Shema kissed him again before turning back towards the window. She looked out over the skyline…right before glancing down on the parking structure below as a squad car, followed by a dark sedan, drove on top of the parking structure.

"WHAT THE HELL?!" Shema pushed Rick out of the way, running to her phone.

"Shema, what's going on?" Rick immediately began getting dressed, glancing down at both cars. He gathered her clothes and brought them to her. "Shema, let me know what's happening." He didn't mean to talk so sternly, but she became silent.

Her screen showed 7 missed calls, and 5 text messages. "Something's wrong."

"Talk to me, Shema."

She could hear Rick, but paused as she opened her messages up.

"Rick… my house caught on fire. My ex-husband has been trying to reach me for the last three hours, because my last alarm code says I was in the house."

Shema ran back to the window, looking down at the two cars. Two police officers got out of the squad car. The door to the sedan opened up, and out comes her ex-husband, Tre, who looks up and points at her office window. She jumped back still completely naked.

"Rick, you have to get out; they're coming up here!"

TO BE CONTINUED IN "LUST" 2019

STAY TUNED FOR
"Maya and Trevor: The Second Experience in Lust."

Coming soon!

Made in the USA
Middletown, DE
18 September 2024

60565695R00019